FURRY AND FLO

capstone
young readers

Furry and Flo is published by
Capstone Young Readers
A Capstone Imprint
1710 Roe Crest Drive
North Mankato, MN 56003
www.capstoneyoungreaders.com

Summary: When an army of skeletons come pouring out of the mysterious basement
crack and start wreaking havoc, it's up to Furry and Flo to deal with the undead army
once and for all!

Library of Congress Cataloging-in-Publication Data is available on the Library of Congress
website.

  ISBN 978-1-4342-6397-1 (library binding) -- ISBN 978-1-62370-048-5 (paper over
board) -- ISBN 978-1-4342-9245-2 (eBook)

Artistic effects: Shutterstock/Kataleks Studio (background)

Book design by Hilary Wacholz

Printed in China.
092013   007733LEOS14

THE
SKELETONS
IN CITY PARK

BOOK 4

BY THOMAS KINGSLEY TROUPE
ILLUSTRATED BY STEPHEN GILPIN

TABLE OF

CONTENTS

SOGGY-JEANS
BLUES

CHAPTER 1

"Oh, c'mon," Flo Gardner said. She reached into the dryer in the basement laundry room at Corman Towers. It was the morning of her first day of school, and her day was already off to a bad start. The jeans she wanted to wear were still damp, along with the rest of the clothes she'd put in the dryer the night before.

Flo yanked her jeans out of the dryer and looked around the dingy laundry room. There was only one other dryer open, so she tossed in the soggy jeans, followed by the rest of the clothes. She added a few more quarters and pressed start.

"What a rip-off," Flo muttered as she hopped up onto the dryer to wait.

Leaning back a bit, Flo glanced at the open space behind the bank of dryers. Up until a few weeks ago, that space had been home to a mysterious blue crack in the floor. Then, she and Furry, her only friend in the building, had leapt through the crack and ended up in Furry's old world — a strange land filled with mummies and other monsters. They'd barely made it back through the portal to their own world before the portal's location shifted.

As soon as they told Curtis, the former building caretaker, what had happened, he'd

gone to work right away. Now, the crack was completely cemented over.

It looks like it was never even there, Flo thought. Maybe this time it'll stay closed for good. I sure hope so. I've dealt with as many creepy creatures as I can handle in one summer.

Even though Flo was keeping her fingers crossed, she remembered what Furry had said. *The crack can't be closed up. Not forever anyway.* After all, they'd tried to cover it up before. Somehow, some way, the monsters from Furry's world managed to come through.

Just then, a man whistling an off-key tune walked into the laundry room holding a toolbox. He had jet-black hair and a thick

mustache. Seeing Flo sitting on top of the dryer, the man smiled. "Hello," he said with a heavy accent. "I am Mr. Panji."

"Hi," Flo said. "Are you the new caretaker?"

10

"Oh, no," Mr. Panji replied, shaking his head. "I am from the repair shop. I am told there is a dryer here that is not feeling so good."

Flo pointed at the dryer that left her load of clothes damp. "It's that one," she said. "You're really fast. I didn't even call —"

"Mrs. Pitzfatrick called last night," Mr. Panji interrupted. He wasted no time in scooting back behind the dryers and getting to work. "Let's see what the trouble is, my friend."

Flo watched the repairman work, smiling as she listened to his off-key whistling. A few times, Mr. Panji's leg crossed over the spot where the crack used to be, making Flo even *more* relieved the cement had been completely sealed up. If it hadn't, there would've been big trouble.

After several minutes, Mr. Panji stood up. He held a big wad of dryer lint in his hand. It was a dark, nasty mess of fluff and string.

"Do you want some of this cotton candy?" Mr. Panji asked. Before Flo could respond, he shook his head. "It is not real, sorry. This is a joke I tell."

The repairman walked around the back of the dryers toward the garbage can. As he did, his foot kicked something, sending it skittering noisily across the floor.

"What is this?" Mr. Panji asked. He bent down to pick up the object and studied it as he threw away the lint ball. "It looks like an old brooch. Is this yours?"

Flo shook her head. "Nope," she said. The only thing she had that she cared about was on the dryer next to her — her Dyno-

Katz lunchbox. It was never far from her side. Today it was fully loaded with a turkey sandwich for her first day of school.

"With your permission, could I have this?" Mr. Panji asked. He held the brooch up so Flo could see it. It looked like a piece of gaudy costume jewelry. A round blue stone was set in a thin gold setting. It was so covered in dust and grime that it barely sparkled.

Flo shrugged. "Sure, why not?" she said. She knew it wasn't hers to give, but she didn't think anyone would  miss the ugly thing. "Whoever owned it probably doesn't live here anymore, anyway."

Mr. Panji nodded and dropped the dusty blue brooch into his jacket pocket. "I shall give it to my wife. She loves antique jewelry. Blue is also her favorite color," he said. "Should anyone ask about it, just have them call my shop."

"Okay, sure," Flo said. She glanced up at the clock, getting a little antsy. If her clothes didn't finish soon, she wouldn't have time for breakfast.

Mr. Panji finished collecting his tools. Then he leaned over and stuck something on the back of the dryer. He stood up, wadded up a small piece of paper, and dropped it into the trash.

"Let me know if any other dryers are feeling sick," Mr. Panji said with a laugh. "And have a good day."

"Sure thing," Flo said and waved. "I will."

As Mr. Panji walked out of the laundry room, the dryer buzzed. Her clothes were dry.

Finally, Flo thought. *At least I won't have to go pants-less on my first day.*

FIRST DAY

CHAPTER 2

Thirty minutes later, Flo was getting on the school bus to Raimi Elementary. "Holy socks," she said as Furry bounded on after her. "I almost didn't recognize you. You're wearing a shirt!"

"Yeah, yeah," Furry mumbled. He flopped down into the seat behind her. "Not my choice. My mom made me. But at least I can tuck my shard inside it."

To prove his point, Furry carefully tucked the blue stone shard tied around his neck inside his navy hoodie and out of sight. As Flo had learned during their last adventure, Furry's shard was more than just a necklace — it was the reason the crack in the laundry room was open in the first place. Furry had used it to open a portal between his world and the human one.

As the bus rattled through the city and made stops at several other apartment buildings, Flo looked around at the other kids.

I wonder if any of them will be my friends, she thought.

Since she and her mom moved around so much, Flo had become an expert at being the new kid. Unfortunately, that didn't necessarily mean she was an expert at making friends. When you moved every few months, it was hard to get too attached to anyone.

Except Furry, Flo thought with a smile.

Flo turned around in her seat. "Are you excited for third grade?" she asked.

Furry shrugged. "Probably as excited as you are for fourth grade," he said. "I'm excited about gym class, though."

Flo glanced around to make sure no one was listening. "You don't do any crazy, like, *werewolf* stunts in gym, do you?" she whispered.

Furry shook his head and waved her off. "Nah," he replied. He paused and then shot her a mischievous grin. "Well, not *too* many, at least."

* * *

When the bus dropped them off in front of Raimi Elementary School, Flo pulled a slip of paper from her lunchbox. She had a letter telling her which classroom she'd been assigned.

"See you later, Flo!" Furry called as he headed upstairs with the rest of the third graders.

Flo waved goodbye and looked around the busy hallway. For the first time since she'd moved to the city, Flo felt alone.

"Are you lost, dear?" a familiar voice asked. "Can I help you?"

Flo glanced up and recognized Ms. Franklin, the school secretary who'd helped her register for school at the beginning of summer. She remembered her being nice. She *also* remembered that Ms. Franklin had called her Florence instead of Flo. She hated that name.

"Uh, yeah," Flo admitted. She adjusted her backpack strap and glanced down at the paper again. "I'm supposed to go to Mrs. Shamp's room. Do you know where that is? It doesn't say which floor or anything."

Ms. Franklin smiled and bent down to look at the letter in Flo's hand. She lifted her old-fashioned glasses and nodded. "Yes," the older woman said. "Go straight down the main hall, past the nurse's office, and take a right at the trophy case. It'll be the first door on your left."

"Okay," Flo said. "Thanks."

"Wait a minute," Ms. Franklin said. "I remember you. You're the girl with the lunchbox."

Flo looked down at her Dyno-Katz lunchbox. It had gotten pretty beat up since the last time she'd been inside the school. Her adventures with Furry had left her prized possession a little more scuffed and dented than she liked.

"Yep, that's me," Flo said with a smile. "Feels like I was just here signing up for school with my mom."

"Summer always seems to fly by. Must've been a good one," Ms. Franklin said, straightening up. "Have a great year, Flo."

"You too," Flo said. She grinned as she headed down the hallway. *Maybe school won't be so bad after all.*

* * *

It didn't take long for Flo to find her new classroom. She walked in just as the bell rang. Her teacher stood in front of the room, talking to a nearly full classroom of kids. The words *MRS. SHAMP* were written in capital letters on the whiteboard.

Mrs. Shamp turned as Flo entered the room. She was a skinny lady with big glasses that made her eyes seem tiny. Her hair was long, dark, and curly.

"Ah, you must be Florence," Mrs. Shamp said. "Come on in. There's a seat for you on the left."

Flo felt her face grow hot as twenty-four pairs of eyes turned to look at her. "Okay," Flo said. She took a deep breath and walked toward the empty seat.

"Oh, and you can leave your lunchbox in your locker," Mrs. Shamp said.

Flo walked over to Mrs. Shamp. "I'd really like to keep my lunchbox close if that's okay," she whispered. "It's really important to me. Also, I don't go by Florence. Everyone calls me Flo."

Mrs. Shamp nodded. "You got it, Flo," she whispered back. "As long as I don't see you dipping into your lunch during class, we shouldn't have any problems."

"Thanks," Flo said quietly. "I like you."

Mrs. Shamp smiled back at her. "I like you, too."

* * *

The rest of Flo's morning went smoothly. Everything seemed to be going well until they started the math unit. Mrs. Shamp had just handed out their workbooks for reviewing fractions when Flo saw something thin and white sneaking past the ground-floor window.

"What was that?" Flo blurted out before she could stop herself.

"Flo?" Mrs. Shamp asked. "Is everything okay?"

Flo looked away from the window and realized everyone was staring at her. *Great,* she thought. *Not only am I the new kid, but I'm the weird new kid.*

"Um, yeah," Flo said quickly. "I just thought I saw something outside."

"Well, if you see it again, let me know," Mrs. Shamp said. "Now you've got me curious."

A few of the kids in the class laughed.

Flo took a deep breath and let it out slowly. She tried to force herself to focus on the instructions for completing the worksheet correctly. But she couldn't help it. She glanced back up at the window.

Flo gasped. There it was again — a skeleton.

NO BONES ABOUT IT

CHAPTER 3

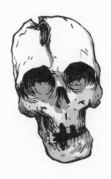

Flo couldn't believe what she was seeing. There, peering through her classroom window, was a skeleton. The creepy thing had a large crack down the center of its skull. Its empty eye sockets were dark, and it was missing the majority of its teeth.

"Whoa," Flo whispered. "Freaky."

Mrs. Shamp turned from the board. "Flo?" the teacher asked. "Are you okay? You look like you've seen a —"

"Skeleton," Flo whispered, pointing to the window. But the skeleton was gone. All she saw outside was the empty playground.

"You saw a skeleton?" a boy asked. "How is that possible?"

"I saw one in a scary movie my brother watched," a girl in the next row added. "It had a sword."

"Class," Mrs. Shamp called. "Let's focus. We all know skeletons exist *inside* our bodies. There aren't any running around outside."

That's what she thinks, Flo thought. *What is happening? I just saw the crack this morning, and it was sealed. With cement!*

"Flo?" Mrs. Shamp called. "Join me up here for a moment, please."

"Okay," Flo said. But she stayed right where she was, her eyes glued to the window.

"Flo," Mrs. Shamp said. "I'm waiting."

"She's probably still looking for skeletons," someone muttered. A few of the kids sitting nearby laughed.

That was enough to snap Flo out of her stupor. She hopped off of her chair and walked toward the front of the room. She felt everyone's eyes on her again.

"Are you feeling okay, Flo?" Mrs. Shamp asked when Flo got close.

Flo shook her head. "Not really," she admitted. She did feel a little hot. Maybe it was from embarrassment. Or maybe it was from seeing a skeleton peeking through the window at her. She wasn't sure.

"We can't have these kinds of interruptions in class," Mrs. Shamp said. "If we do, we'll never get our work done."

"I know," Flo said. "I'm sorry. I just thought I saw something out there."

"A skeleton?" Mrs. Shamp asked.

Flo nodded.

"It would be cool if you did, huh?" Mrs. Shamp said, smiling. "But you and I both know that kind of thing doesn't really happen."

If you only knew, Flo thought. But since she couldn't exactly tell her teacher about the giant spiders, goblins, and mummies she'd battled over the summer, Flo nodded again.

"So do we have a deal?" Mrs. Shamp asked. "No more outbursts?"

"Yes," Flo said.

Mrs. Shamp smiled, and Flo forced herself to smile back. But something wasn't right, and Flo wished more than ever that Furry was in her class.

Flo managed to make it through the rest of the morning with no more skeleton sightings. By the time lunch rolled around, she was starting to wonder if she *had* just imagined it after all.

Maybe I'm losing it, Flo thought as she walked into the cafeteria. She took a seat at a table by herself. Within minutes, a figure appeared next to her.

"I thought I smelled you over here," Furry said.

"Okay, geez," Flo muttered, glancing around. "Not so loud. People are going to know you're a werewolf."

"Nah, they'll just think you smell," Furry said with a wink. He tossed his bagged lunch onto the table and took a seat next to Flo. He

opened his bag, pulled out his chips and juice box, and dug in.

After a few minutes of chewing, Furry stopped stuffing his face long enough to say, "So, I think we have problem."

Flo closed her eyes. She had a bad feeling that she knew *exactly* what problem Furry was talking about. It was the same one she'd seen creeping past her classroom window.

"Earth to Flo. Did you hear me?" Furry asked as he took a drink of his juice.

"I heard you," Flo said, opening her eyes. "Skeletons, right?"

Furry nodded. "Yeah, skeletons. A lot of them. How did you know?"

Flo leaned closer to her friend so she wouldn't be overheard. "I saw one outside my classroom window earlier," she whispered. "But what are we supposed to do about it? We're in school!"

"I know," Furry whispered back. "But we're the only ones who know how to handle this kind of thing."

Flo opened her lunchbox and studied the picture of her and her dad taped inside the lid. She never went anywhere without that lunchbox. It reminded her of her dad, and her dad had always told her she should do what was right, no matter what.

I wonder if that includes getting in trouble at school to stop skeletons from taking over the city, Flo thought.

Flo closed her lunchbox. There was no way she could eat now. Not knowing that there were skeletons roaming free. "That stupid crack," she muttered.

"How do you know it's the crack?" Furry asked.

"Well, what else could it be?" Flo said. "That thing is nothing but trouble, I swear."

"I know," Furry said, finishing the last of his chips. "And it's all my fault."

Flo hated to admit it, but Furry was sort of right. When he'd used his portal shard to escape from his world as a young werewolf, he'd left a pathway open between their two worlds. As Flo had learned during an unplanned trip back to Furry's world, it was the portal shard that had been keeping the crack in the basement laundry room open. And as long as the crack stayed open, anything from Furry's world could sneak through the crack to wreak havoc in her world.

Still, Flo knew that if it came down to a choice between losing her best friend and closing the crack, she'd rather have Furry here. She took a deep breath and forced herself to ask, "So what do we do?"

HALL PASS

CHAPTER 4

When Flo returned to class after lunch, her stomach felt like it was full of butterflies. She and Furry had decided to meet in the hallway at 1:35, but now that she was alone again, she was having doubts about their plan. And she really wasn't looking forward to taking on a bunch of skeletons.

First the mummy, now the skeletons, Flo thought with a shudder. *All this undead stuff gives me the creeps.*

Mrs. Shamp was talking about learning to read maps, but Flo barely heard her. She kept her eyes on the window. She hadn't seen another skeleton since that morning. *Maybe we got lucky and someone else took care of the problem*, she thought. *Maybe they're already back where they belong.*

Mrs. Shamp pointed to a giant world map tacked to the bulletin board. "Can anyone tell me what the little box with the symbols on a map is called?" she asked.

"A legend," someone replied.

Flo looked up at the clock nervously. She was supposed to leave to meet Furry any second. As the second hand swept past the seven, Flo's stomach started to rumble nervously.

It was time.

Flo raised her hand. "Um, excuse me, Mrs. Shamp? Could I have the hall pass?"

Mrs. Shamp turned to face her. "Are you feeling okay, Flo?" the teacher asked. "You look a little pale."

"I do?" Flo asked.

Mrs. Shamp nodded and went to her desk. She rifled through the top drawer and came up with a small spiral notepad. She wrote something down, tore off the rectangular piece of paper, and handed it to Flo. "Did you eat anything at lunch?" she asked.

"No," Flo admitted. "I wasn't hungry."

"You don't look like you feel very well," Mrs. Shamp said. "Why don't you go down to the nurse's office and lie down for a bit? Make sure you bring your lunchbox with you and eat something."

"Okay," Flo said, feeling a little less nervous. Now she wouldn't have to worry about being back right away. With a note for the nurse, she could leave the classroom, find Furry, and head out to stop the monsters.

Again.

"I'll call down to the nurse's office and let her know you're coming," Mrs. Shamp said. She picked up the classroom phone, punched a few numbers, and talked to the school nurse on the other line.

Rats, Flo thought. *There goes that plan.*

* * *

Furry was waiting in the hallway when Flo walked out. "Whoa," he said. "You look like you're going to barf, Flo."

"I know," Flo said. "That's why I have to go to the nurse's office."

"Are you kidding?" Furry shook his head. "We don't have time for that. I just saw a bunch of skeletons hiding behind the bushes across the street. More and more are appearing every minute!"

"Has anyone else seen them yet?" Flo asked.

"I don't think so, but if we don't do something, the whole city will be full of them!" Furry said. He motioned to a side door. "Let's go out this way. If we hurry, no one will ever know we're gone!"

Flo ignored him and started walking down the hallway toward the nurse's office.

"Hey, where are you going?" Furry said.

"The nurse's office," Flo said. "Maybe I can have them call my mom to pick me up. That way, I won't get in trouble for sneaking out of school on my first day."

Furry shook his head. "That won't work!" he insisted. "If you're sick, your mom is going to make you stay in bed."

Flo sighed. Furry had a point. She looked up and down the empty hallway. If they left now, no one would see them go. But the school nurse was expecting her. If she didn't show up . . .

"Flo Gardner?" a voice called from down the hallway. Flo turned to find a woman wearing a white shirt and dark cotton pants. She was waving to her.

"Nurse's office it is," Flo whispered.

* * *

A few minutes later, Flo sat on the small, paper-covered cot near the window in the nurse's office. The school nurse, a pretty lady named Janice, took her temperature.

"Well, you don't have a fever," the nurse said.

"I didn't eat anything today," Flo said. "I felt kind of dizzy after lunch."

Janice sat on a short stool and studied Flo. "Do you feel up to eating now?" she asked.

Flo shrugged. "I guess," she said. "I mostly feel tired, though."

The nurse nodded understandingly. "It's not easy being the new kid, is it?" she said. "You probably just have a nervous stomach, and if you don't eat anything, you won't feel so hot. Do you have your lunch with you?"

Flo nodded and opened her Dyno-Katz lunchbox. She took out a turkey sandwich — her specialty. Flo prided herself on making the best turkey sandwiches of anyone, kid or adult. And she never left home without one.

"Tell you what, why don't you eat your sandwich and lie down for a little bit?" Janice suggested. "Some rest will do you good."

Flo glanced up at the window near her cot, feeling a little guilty about what she was about to do. "Yeah," she said. "Okay."

Janice opened the door to the room and looked back at Flo. "I'll check back in on you later, okay? You won't miss much," she said with a wink. "The first day of school is usually the easiest."

Clearly none of her *first days have involved skeletons*, Flo thought.

INFESTED!

CHAPTER 5

As soon as the door closed and she was sure the nurse wasn't coming back, Flo carefully slid the window open. Lucky for her, the nurse's office was on the first floor. She climbed out the open window as quietly as she could, careful not to clank her lunchbox against the window frame.

Flo dropped to the ground outside, her heart pounding like a drum in her chest. She

was almost more nervous about leaving school than she was about dealing with the skeletons. *Where are all of these skeletons, anyway?* she wondered.

Just then, a flash of navy blue caught her eye. An instant later, Furry stood next to her.

"Let me guess," Flo muttered. "You could smell that I was over here."

"Yeah," Furry said with a wide smile. "Werewolf senses are awesome. Now let's get moving before someone notices we're gone."

Furry and Flo cautiously headed toward
the fence surrounding the school property.
In a single leap, Furry was on the other side.
It took Flo a moment to climb over and join
him. Once they'd made it off school property
undetected, Flo glanced around. She didn't
see anything out of the ordinary. No skeletons
roaming free. No one screaming for help. No
cars crashing into fire hydrants.

"I don't see anything," Flo said. "Maybe they went home." She hated to risk getting in trouble for nothing.

But Furry was already heading toward the street. "I don't think so," he said. "There are lots of them out here. I saw a bunch from the second-floor window. Plus I can smell them."

"Ooh, what do they smell —" Flo started to ask. Then she remembered the mummy they'd had to deal with. It had stunk something fierce. She *definitely* didn't want to think about that again. She shook her head. "Never mind. I don't want to know."

"We should head back home and see what happened to the crack," Furry said.

"Fine," Flo said. "Let's hurry up before the nurse notices I'm gone. The last thing I need is to get in trouble on my first day."

Just then, a beat-up yellow pickup truck screeched around the corner. The driver jammed on the brakes and left a thick layer of black skid marks on the road. "Ferdinand, is that you?" the driver shouted out the window.

Flo looked closer at the old man in the driver's seat and recognized Curtis Rockwell, the retired caretaker at Corman Towers.

"Hey, Curtis," Furry said.

"Don't you 'Hey, Curtis' me," Curtis snapped. "Get in, you two. We've got problems back home!"

Furry and Flo scrambled in through the passenger-side door, and Curtis hit the gas. In seconds, the truck was racing toward Corman Towers. Flo couldn't buckle her seatbelt fast enough. Outside her window, traffic and people on the street whipped by in a blur.

"I told you to quit messing with that seal," Curtis said, glaring at Furry.

"I didn't mess with it!" Furry cried. "How could I? You cemented it shut!"

Curtis honked his horn and veered to the left, sending Flo careening into Furry. "With that portal-cutter thing," he said. "You could have easily opened the seal back up."

Flo groaned. The portal shard. That thing was more trouble than it was worth. Still, she knew if Furry tossed it through the crack and closed it for good, he'd never be able to go back to his world. And he wasn't ready to do that.

"I didn't do it," Furry insisted. "I'm only wearing the shard to keep it safe! You gotta believe me, Curtis!"

Flo's shoes rustled the fast-food wrappers and cups on the floor. She wondered what they'd find back at the apartment building. *Judging by the way Curtis is driving, probably nothing good*, she thought.

"Have you seen these skeleton things before?" Flo asked.

"Yeah," Furry admitted. "Just once, though. They're called the Bone Horde back home.

They do people's dirty work for them. They can appear and disappear on command. Whoever holds the Bone Talisman controls the Bone Horde."

"So who's controlling them?" Flo asked. "And why can't we find them?"

"Oh, I found them, all right," Curtis muttered. "You should see the mess back at the apartments."

* * *

Moments later, Curtis screeched to a stop in front of Corman Towers. They all jumped out of Curtis's truck and raced to the side entrance. They scrambled down the steps into the basement hallway and turned the corner to the laundry room door.

There was a shovel wedged under the doorknob to hold it closed.

"You kids might want to back up," Curtis warned them. He reached out and pulled the shovel away. The door immediately swung open.

As soon as she saw what was inside, Flo gasped. The laundry room was crowded with skeletons. When the Bone Horde realized the door was open, they immediately surged toward the door, swiping with their bony fingers as they tried to claw their way out.

"Back up!" Curtis shouted, swinging the shovel with all his might. He connected with one of the skeletons, knocking it into a pile of bones. Ribs, a clavicle, and a tibia bounced off of the washing machines and dryers.

In the hallway, Flo turned to Furry and watched as her friend plugged his nose and blew to make his ears pop. Gray hair

instantly exploded across Furry's skin as he transformed into a werewolf. He tore through his shirt and split his pants in two spots. As soon as he was fully wolfed out, Furry leapt into the room, growling and snapping at another skeleton.

"We have to keep them inside!" Curtis yelled as he smacked another skeleton to bits. He kicked the disassembled bones away and dodged a skeletal hand.

Flo watched helplessly from the hallway as Curtis and Furry battled the Bone Horde. Then she suddenly remembered something and didn't feel so useless after all. "Holy socks!" she cried. "I think I know what happened!"

THE
BONE
TALISMAN

CHAPTER 6

Flo ducked as a skull sailed across the room and smashed against the doorframe. The jawbone came apart and clattered across the floor.

"Furry!" she yelled across the bony battle. "What does that Bone Talisman thing look like?"

Furry bit into a leg bone, tugged, and let the rest of the skeleton topple to pieces before answering. "I don't know," he growled through his teeth. "It's got a jewel of some sort. Kind of shiny?"

Just like what the repair guy found this morning! Flo thought. Had that piece of junk he'd found behind the dryer slipped out of the crack before Curtis sealed it up? It seemed possible. After all, stranger things had *definitely* happened at Corman Towers in the past. Flo could vouch for that.

Flo grinned. "I think I know who has it!" she hollered. But the boys were too busy battling the well-armed skeletons to pay much attention.

"Goodnight!" Curtis yelled. He smacked the last skeleton in the hipbone and watched it crumble to the floor. With all the skeleton remains strewn around, it looked like

Halloween had exploded all over the laundry room.

"This isn't all of them," Furry said. "There are more out in the city."

"I know," Curtis said. He used the shovel to scoop up as many bones as he could. "And there'll be more coming through any moment. Come over here, you two."

Flo carefully tiptoed past the piles of shattered skeletons and followed Furry and Curtis to the hidden space behind the dryers. She wasn't the least bit surprised at what she saw.

There were chunks of concrete all over the floor. The nice cement work Curtis had done was gone, replaced with a jagged, glowing crack in the floor. The seal had split, and the portal back to Furry's world was open once more.

"Oh, great," Furry said. "That means there are more skeletons on their way. Until they're told to stop, they're just going to keep coming."

Flo grinned, proud of herself for solving their problem. "Then we're in luck," she said. "I know who has the Bone Talisman."

"Who?" Furry asked.

Flo couldn't remember his name. "Some guy who came to fix the dryer," she said. "I met him this morning. He had really dark hair and a mustache."

Curtis groaned. "That doesn't narrow it down much," he said. "Can you remember anything else? We've used twenty different repair services over the years."

Flo thought about it. "He was really bad at whistling," she said. "Like, terrible."

A rumbling sound suddenly came from deep within the crack, and it glowed brighter blue.

"Great," Curtis said. "Sounds like we're about to have more company!"

A skull suddenly popped through the crack in the floor. Curtis quickly wound up and

clonked it on the head with
his shovel, knocking it back
into Furry's world.

"We need to find
that thing," Curtis said.
"And quick. I can't
hold these things
off forever.
Besides,
I've got my
afternoon
programs to watch."

"Can you remember anything else about
that guy?" Furry asked. "Dark hair and bad
whistling isn't really much to go on."

Flo tried to think. The man had asked if
the brooch belonged to anyone. He'd collected
his tools. Then . . .

"He threw something in the garbage!" Flo said. "Some lint and something else. Maybe there's a clue in there."

Flo ran to the garbage can and started digging. Finally she unearthed the giant lint ball and a crumpled piece of waxy paper. "Got it," she hollered. She flattened it out and saw it was blank.

"Great, it's blank," Furry said. "That doesn't help us at all."

Flo shook her head. "It's the back of a sticker," she said. "He must've put a sticker on the dryer he fixed!"

Flo hurried back over to the row of dryers and crouched down next to Furry and Curtis. Furry pointed a hairy paw to a small red service sticker clinging to the back of the troublesome dryer. The words *SERVICED BY*

PANJI & SON REPAIR were clearly printed. The shop's phone number and address were listed below.

"This is it!" Furry shouted. "He's close by. I can almost smell him."

"That was my next idea, Sniffy," Flo said. She looked up at the clock on the laundry room wall. They'd been gone from school for way too long. She hoped the nurse hadn't gone back to check on her. But as nervous as she was about getting in trouble, Flo knew they couldn't go back to school yet.

"Get moving and find this guy and that medallion thing," Curtis ordered. "It sounds like a ton of them are coming through."

Curtis grabbed the shovel again and stood guard over the glowing crack while Furry and Flo raced out the door.

MR. PANJI'S
PICNIC

CHAPTER 7

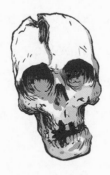

Flo grabbed her bike from the storage room and headed for the side door. Furry bounded up the stairs behind her, still in his werewolf form. They needed to move quickly if they hoped to stop the Bone Horde before they caused too much damage.

It was hard to steer with her Dyno-Katz lunchbox in hand, but Flo never went anywhere without her lunchbox, so she tried to make the best of it. Furry did his best to look like a dog — a dog running in a pair of torn shorts and a hooded sweatshirt.

"C'mon," Furry pleaded. He seemed eager to turn up the speed and get to the repair shop, but he waited for Flo.

"I haven't seen any skeletons out here yet," Flo said, ignoring Furry's need for speed. "Maybe the talisman isn't working."

Furry shook his head, sniffing the air. "No, they're here in the city," he barked. "I can smell them. But I can't tell where."

Flo hopped her bike over the curb to cross the next street. *At least the sidewalks aren't too crowded*, she thought. *If all those skeletons were out here, we'd have some serious explaining to do.*

Furry suddenly came to a stop right across from City Park. "We're here," he said.

Flo braked next to him and hopped off her bike. Sure enough, the window next to them had the words *PANJI & SON Repair* stenciled in chipped, faded letters. A sign on the door read: *OPEN — COME ON IN!*

Flo took a deep breath. She watched Furry pretend to sniff a fire hydrant.

"Should I just go in, or . . ." Flo's voice trailed off as someone inside the store flipped the sign around so that it read: *CLOSED — PLEASE CALL AGAIN SOON!*

"Oh, no!" Flo said.

Furry glanced over from the fire hydrant. She watched him sniff the air.

Just then, the front door of the repair shop opened. Furry and Flo quickly ducked behind a car as Mr. Panji and a woman exited. The repairman's dark hair had been neatly combed. He held the woman's hand and carried a picnic basket with his free hand. The woman wore a nice skirt and a dark sweater.

That must be his wife, Flo thought.

"It's a perfect day for the park, my dear," Mr. Panji said.

"Is that him?" Furry whispered.

Flo nodded and watched as Mr. and Mrs. Panji crossed the street. Mr. Panji whistled slightly off-key as the couple continued along the path toward City Park with their picnic basket.

Furry peered between two cars and watched them disappear into the trees. "Well, I can tell you one thing," he said. "Getting this talisman back won't be a picnic."

Flo groaned and rolled her eyes at the terrible pun. "Can we save the jokes for later?" she said. "We have a talisman to find."

Flo looked both ways and quickly pushed her bike across the street. Furry followed after her and together they headed down the same path the Panjis had taken. They spotted the couple sitting on a fleece blanket and eating their picnic lunch.

"Do you think he has the talisman with him?" Furry asked quietly. He watched the couple like a hungry beast eyeing his next meal. Flo knew Furry was a vegetarian, but the look in his eyes was definitely saying something else.

"Well, he said he wanted to give the brooch to his wife," Flo whispered back.

As Furry and Flo watched, Mr. Panji reached into his pocket and pulled out a small, round object. When his hand opened, the bright blue stone glinted in the late summer sun.

"That's it," Flo hissed and grabbed a fistful of Furry's fur in excitement. The werewolf let out a little yelp of surprise, and they both ducked behind a giant tree as Mr. Panji turned to look their way.

When they peeked out again, Flo's heart almost stopped. Emerging from the line of trees and marching straight toward Mr. and Mrs. Panji was the Bone Horde.

"D-d-do you s-s-see what —" Flo stammered.

"Yeah," Furry interrupted. "There they are."

Before the Panjis could catch sight of the skeleton army marching their way, Furry ran toward them. He growled and barked as he closed in on the poor picnickers. Mr. and Mrs. Panji quickly stood up and bolted toward the park path.

Flo hopped on her bike, adjusted her lunchbox in her hand, and chased after Furry and the fleeing couple. She was grateful they hadn't noticed the skeletons appearing from nowhere. But as she rode past their blanket and basket, Flo felt bad. *So much for their nice picnic*, she thought.

PARK

PURSUIT

CHAPTER 8

What's he doing? Flo wondered as she watched Furry snap at the Panjis' heels. She knew Furry could run twice as fast, but it seemed like the werewolf was holding back. Glancing behind her, Flo saw the skeletons were crowding the park's path.

"Furry!" Flo cried. "Do something! They're coming!"

"Someone call for help!" Mr. Panji shouted. "This dog in pants wants to bite us!"

The werewolf growled again, making the poor couple cry out in fear. Flo felt awful. Their romantic picnic had been ruined, and now a nine-year-old werewolf was scaring them half to death.

I hope he knows what he's doing, Flo thought. She could hear the *click-clack* of bony feet on the pavement close behind her.

Up ahead, Mr. Panji still grasped the talisman in his fingers. It glinted gold and blue in the sun. Furry's head bobbed up and down in time with Mr. Panji's swaying hand. As his hand swung back, Furry surged forward and licked Mr. Panji's wrist. The slobbery

kiss caught the man off guard, and he let go of the brooch.

Furry quickly snatched it up before it hit the sidewalk and closed his werewolf lips around it. Almost instantly, the sound of clattering feet ceased. Flo turned, glancing down the path once more. Every one of the skeletons had disappeared.

Furry darted off the path and through the trees. Mr. and Mrs. Panji, unaware they were no longer being chased, continued fleeing through the park.

Flo steered her bike off the path after Furry, jumping over exposed roots and veering around rocks. The contents of her lunchbox rattled with every bump. She blasted through some prickly bushes and into a small, grassy clearing where Furry stood on all fours.

"What happened?" Flo asked. "All of the skeletons just disappeared. Did you tell the talisman to do that?"

Furry shook his head, but looked around cautiously. "Day dill ear," he mumbled. He had the Bone Talisman in his mouth, which made it hard for Flo to understand him.

"What did you say?" She hopped off her bike and laid it down on the ground. "Spit that thing out before you swallow it, okay?"

Furry did as he was told and dropped the talisman onto the grass. "I said they're still here," he said in a clearer voice. "And they're close."

As if on cue, the clearing was suddenly surrounded by skeletons. In the time it took Flo to blink, they were everywhere. Some wore helmets, while others had leather belts tied

around their exposed bones. A few had pieces
of armor affixed to their arms and legs, while
still others carried shields. The ones with the
rusty swords made Flo especially nervous.

"Yikes!" Flo exclaimed, backing away from
the edge of the trees. She huddled closer
to Furry, both of them eyeing the skeletons
carefully. None of them made a move. "How
did they appear again?"

"I don't know," Furry whispered. A low growl began to rumble in his throat. "I didn't tell them to."

Flo hadn't said anything either. She stepped back again and a flash of metal caught her eye. At her feet, she saw the talisman shining in the sun and bent down to pick it up. "Oh gross, Furry," she said with a groan. "It's all slobbery."

Flo turned toward the shade and used the edge of her shirt to wipe off the werewolf spit. As she rubbed the talisman, the skeletons briefly disappeared.

Seconds later, they were back as if they'd always been there.

"What did you do, Flo?" Furry cried.

"I don't . . ." Flo started to say. Then she realized something. "I think it's the sun! Watch!"

To prove her point, Flo turned back so that the talisman was in the shade once again. Instantly, the skeletons disappeared. When she turned around again and let the sun hit the brooch, the skeletons immediately reappeared in the clearing.

"That explains why we didn't see them out here until the repairman pulled out the talisman," Furry said. "His pocket kept it out of the sun!"

"He must have taken it out while we were in school, too," Flo said. "That would explain why they were lurking around my classroom window."

The entire Bone Horde army just stood there with their empty eyes. They seemed to be awaiting a command. A chill raced up Flo's back and she held the talisman up to the sun. As she did, she noticed a secret etching in the sapphire. When the sun hit it just right, she saw a faint carving that looked like a skull.

"Well, this isn't so bad," Flo said. "At least they didn't attack us."

The words had barely left her mouth when the Bone Horde sprang into action. They ran toward Furry and Flo with their arms raised and jaws open in a silent battle cry.

SURROUNDED!

CHAPTER 9

Flo tried to grab her bike but found herself yanked back by a furry paw.

"There's no time!" Furry shouted as the skeletons closed in. "We have to run for it!"

Flo sprinted with Furry toward the edge of the trees and down another narrow path. *We're never going to make it back to school at this rate*, she thought.

"What are we doing?" she hollered as they ran. "We just need to cover up the talisman!"

Flo stopped in her tracks and shaded the talisman to block out the sun. But the skeletons just kept coming. Not a single one of them flickered or showed any signs of disappearing . . . or stopping.

"Uh-oh," Flo said as they tore off down the path once more.

"Maybe they can't disappear in attack mode," Furry suggested, plowing through the underbrush on all fours. "What did you say to make them come after us, anyway?"

"I don't know!" Flo replied. "Something about being glad that they weren't attacking us?"

"Maybe they only heard the last part! They must have thought it was a command since you were holding the talisman when you said it!" Furry said.

"Great, now I'm afraid to say anything ever again!" Flo yelled.

"Well, you'd better say something to get them to back off!" Furry growled.

"Okay," Flo cried. She was short of breath, but raised the talisman skyward. "Hey, boneheads! No more attacking!"

But Flo's newest command just made the skeletons crazier. They swiped and clawed at the ground with their bony hands. The

skeletons wielding swords swung them back and forth, slicing low-hanging branches from trees.

"Yeah, that didn't work," Flo muttered.

In the distance, she heard dogs barking. The thick cover of trees in the park kept them hidden for the time being, but Flo knew they'd soon spill out near the fenced-in area where people let their dogs run free.

"We must be close to the dog park," Flo shouted. "What are we going to do? We can't lead these guys to the people out there."

Furry barked and howled in excitement. "You just gave me the best idea ever! Get those skeletons to follow you back toward the clearing."

"What? Are you crazy?" Flo shook her head. "They'll get me!"

Furry just smiled. "Trust me," he said. "I'll be back before you know it."

Before Flo could protest, Furry took off like a gray streak through the woods. Flo rounded a cluster of trees and headed back. "This is dumb," she groaned. "I should be in school."

But Flo knew there was no other choice. She held the talisman high and gave the Bone Horde their next command. "Come get me, you hollow heads," Flo shouted.

The skeletons immediately moved toward Flo with their bony arms outstretched. Flo leapt over a rotted fallen tree and took off running toward the clearing. By the time she got there, she was tired and out of breath.

"This is the worst . . . plan . . . ever," Flo gasped. She spotted her bike on the ground where she'd left it, but she was too tired to try to ride off on it. She tripped and fell, landing inches from the back tire.

When Flo sat up, she saw skeletons closing in from all sides. They had her completely surrounded, forming a circle of bones ready for battle. *This is it*, she thought desperately. *I'm going to get eaten by a bunch of skeletons.*

Flo swung her lunchbox back and forth, catching the closest skeleton in the shin. The

blow shattered the skeleton's leg, and down it went. The bone warrior managed to catch itself with its hands and crawled forward, snapping his teeth at the cuff of Flo's jeans.

"Get out of here!" Flo cried, hoping for any command that would get the skeletons to leave her alone.

But nothing seemed to work. One skeleton grabbed her leg, while another scratched her arm with a bony finger. Flo swung her lunchbox again and again, knocking bones loose, but it wasn't enough. They kept coming.

Flo screamed and covered her face with her arms. Just as she prepared to become a skeleton snack, she heard the stampede of a hundred small feet approaching.

GIVE A DOG A BONE

CHAPTER 10

Furry howled a long, loud battle cry. The echo of other howls ringing through City Park soon joined his. There were big barks and small yelps. When Flo opened her eyes, she couldn't believe it — there were dogs everywhere!

In moments, the skeletons were engaged in battle with a new enemy. This time their foes had fur, sharp teeth, and a taste for bones.

"Where did these guys come from?" Flo shouted, picking herself up off the ground.

"The dog park!" Furry shouted. The werewolf leapt in the air and locked his jaws onto a skeleton's ribcage. He jerked his head sideways, tossing the bone warrior into one of his fellow soldiers. Both skeletons clattered apart in a heap of limbs.

Flo watched in amazement as a bulldog tackled another skeleton, knocking its skull loose from the spinal column. A pair of poodles began chewing on another skeleton's arms and legs. Everywhere she looked, dogs fought off the Bone Horde.

Flo grinned. It was the perfect army to sic on the bony minions. She turned and ducked as a skeleton's rusty sword swished over her head.

"Oooh," Flo gasped, realizing how close a call that had been. She swung her lunchbox and slammed the skeleton right in the jawbone. A handful of teeth dropped out of the skeleton's mouth. Still on its feet, it swung again at Flo. She raised her lunchbox up and blocked the sword's blow. A large dent creased the box's lid.

All right that does it, Flo fumed. *Now I'm mad.*

With a screech, she cocked her arm back and swung the Dyno-Katz lunchbox with everything she had. It connected with the skeleton's clavicle, loosening both arms at once. With a well-placed kick, she blasted the warrior's pelvis. The bone soldier dropped into a pile of pieces.

"*Bone* appétit," Flo said with a snarl.

Furry thrashed another skeleton back and forth by the leg. He dragged it over to the tree and with a heave, launched it against the tree's trunk. The skeleton exploded in a shower of bones.

"They keep rebuilding themselves and coming at us!" Furry shouted.

"Are you serious?" Flo cried. "Knocking them apart isn't enough?" She remembered poor Curtis back at the apartment building. If the skeletons were coming back together, he really had his hands full. Flo had to do something quickly.

"I think we have to destroy that talisman!" Furry shouted.

Flo looked down at the talisman in her hand. *I hope this works*, she thought. She threw it on the ground, stomped on it, and picked it up again. The talisman remained undamaged. When she looked around, the skeletons and dogs continued to battle.

"It won't break!" Flo said. "I don't know how to get these guys to stop fighting."

Instantly, all of the skeleton warriors froze in place.

"Hey!" Furry let out a howl of excitement. "What did you do?"

Flo tossed the talisman in the air and caught it. She smiled, like she'd known what she was doing all along. "I just said to —"

"Better yet," Furry interrupted, "don't say anything!"

Flo nodded. As long as she held the troublesome Bone Talisman, she didn't know what her words would make the skeletons do next.

Furry looked in the direction of the dog park. "Their owners will be here any minute, looking for them," he cried. "We have to clean this mess up before anyone sees it."

Flo nodded. "Yeah. I don't want to explain a park full of skeleton bones."

Furry barked three times, and the dogs all gathered around. They sat in a group and watched the werewolf intently as he barked at

them. The other dogs seemed to be absorbing his every word. A golden retriever near the back looked familiar to Flo, but she couldn't figure out where she'd seen him before.

A moment later, Furry barked a final bark. "Hop on your bike, Flo," the little werewolf said quickly. "They're going to follow you back to the apartment building."

"Um . . . okay," Flo said. She opened her lunchbox and dropped the talisman inside. With a tug, she pulled her bike up, threw her leg over, and started pedaling toward the main path. When she glanced back, she saw a parade of dogs trotting closely behind her. Each one carried a pile of bones in its mouth.

"Come on, dogs," Flo called, finally catching on to Furry's plan. "I know a great spot to bury those!"

* * *

In no time at all, Flo and the dogs

arrived at the apartment's service entrance.

She propped open the door and led them

downstairs to the laundry room. She shoved

it open to find Curtis inside, sweeping bones

into the crack.

"Hoo boy," Curtis cried. He adjusted his

thick glasses and wiped his sweaty forehead

with the edge of his shirt. "I don't know what you kids did, but those skeletons finally gave up the fight."

Flo shrugged. "I just told them to stop," she said. "Simple."

Just then, the parade of dogs came through the doorway.

"Oh, and we brought the pieces with us to put back where they belong," Flo said. She led the dogs to the crack. After more barked orders from Furry, the dogs dropped the disassembled Bone Horde back into the blue crack in the floor piece by piece.

WHOOSH! WHOOSH! WHOOSH!

Once all of the bones were gone, Flo opened her Dyno-Katz lunchbox and pulled out the Bone Talisman. "I should probably throw this in too, huh?"

"Definitely," Furry agreed. He grabbed a juice box from Flo's lunchbox and drained the drink in three quick swallows. When it was gone, he let out a loud belch and transformed back into his human form.

"Geez," Flo said. "I don't know if I'll ever get used to that." She studied the Bone Talisman for another moment before tossing it into the glowing crack. "See you later, suckers."

WHOOSH!

FINAL
NOTE

CHAPTER 11

With the Bone Horde back where they belonged, Curtis helped Furry and Flo load the helpful dogs into the back of his truck. As they drove back toward the dog park, Furry turned to Flo in the front seat. "Sorry I left you alone with the Bone Horde," he said.

Flo shook her head. "Don't worry about it. I'm just glad you and the dogs got there in time! A little sooner would've been better, though," she said with a grin.

Furry smiled back. "Some of the dogs didn't want to go," he said. "And their owners weren't too happy with me, either."

Thankfully, the owners changed their tunes when Furry and Flo brought their pets back to them. Since no one recognized human Furry as the dog that had led their pets astray, the people treated the three of them like they were heroes. They thanked Curtis, Furry, and Flo for bringing their pets back safe and sound.

When Flo saw the golden retriever's owner, she suddenly remembered where she'd seen him before. "Was that the dog you saved from getting hit by the taxi a while back?" Flo whispered.

"Yeah," Furry said with a grin. "Rocky owed me a favor. We're even now."

Once the truck was empty and every dog was accounted for, Flo looked at her watch. They'd been gone from school for way too long. *Uh-oh*, she thought. *We're in major trouble.*

"Um, Curtis," Flo said. "Do you think you could give us a ride back to school?"

* * *

Back at Raimi Elementary, Furry snuck in through the front door, still holding his hall pass. Flo ran along the side of the school as quickly and quietly as possible. In moments she found the window to the nurse's office and peeked in. The cot with the crinkled paper on it was just like she'd left it.

"Perfect," Flo whispered. She set her lunchbox down for a moment and tried the window. It didn't budge.

Uh-oh, she thought. She tried again and again, straining her muscles, but it was no use. The window was locked. When she looked up again, she saw Janice, the school nurse, standing in the window looking out at her.

Flo smiled and waved sheepishly. "Um, hi?" she said.

* * *

Flo got into a whole mess of trouble that night at home. The nurse had called her mom and told her all about Flo's first-day disappearing act. As punishment for sneaking out, Flo wasn't allowed to watch TV for a month.

"I'm really disappointed in you, Flo," Mom said over dinner that night. "This is *not* the right way to start off at a new school. You know better."

"I said I'm sorry, Mom," Flo said, looking down and picking at her fish sticks. "I won't do it again, I promise."

"I know you won't," her mom said. "I just don't understand why you felt the need to leave school in the middle of the day."

Flo was quiet. She couldn't tell her mom about the skeletons, or the Bone Talisman, or that Furry had been involved. Instead, she just shrugged. "I don't know," she whispered. "It was dumb."

When Flo refused to explain why she'd left school, her mom sent her to her room. When she still wouldn't talk, Mom sent Flo to do the laundry.

"When the load is washed and dried, you'll fold it, put it away, and go to bed," Mom said.

"But Mom, it'll only be like seven o'clock!" Flo protested.

Her mom insisted and pointed to the door. Flo could tell from the look on her face that arguing wouldn't get her anywhere, so she gathered up the dirty clothes and trudged down to the basement laundry room.

Thirty minutes later, Flo sat on top of one of the washing machines as it ran through the rinse cycle. She was angry at just about everything.

Stupid skeletons, stupid crack, stupid locked window, Flo thought. She wanted to tell her mom what had happened, but she knew she couldn't. It was too dangerous for Mom or anyone to know about the crack. Plus, it was Furry's secret to share, not hers.

Furry suddenly appeared in the doorway. "Hey," he said. "Are you okay?"

Flo scowled. She didn't feel like talking to anyone at the moment — not even her best friend.

"Did you get in trouble?" Furry asked. He wore only a pair of shorts and had the portal shard necklace around his neck. He held something behind his back.

Flo kept quiet.

"I'm really sorry," Furry continued. "But at least we stopped them. It could've gotten ugly if those boneheads were tearing through the city. You know?"

"Yeah," Flo muttered. "I guess. But couldn't we have at least waited until after school? Then maybe my mom wouldn't be so mad at me."

Furry shrugged. "By then it might've been too late."

Flo was quiet again. She stared at the floor.

"I brought you an orange Popsicle," Furry said, pulling

his hand out from behind his back. "It's the last one."

When Flo didn't respond, he looked upset. "Are you mad at me?" he asked.

"No," Flo said. "I'm just mad that it's *our* job to keep the bad stuff out. I think it's getting worse."

Furry nodded. "Yeah. I sometimes think I should just go back to where I belong. Let the portal seal itself up."

"No!" Flo cried. "You can't!"

"I might have to," Furry said. "If the portal stays open, who knows what will come out of there next! I'm making your world dangerous just by being here."

"I know," Flo said. "But still . . ."

Furry looked at Flo with his eyebrows raised.

"I don't want you to go," Flo whispered.

Furry opened his mouth to say something when a sharp *CRACK!* suddenly sounded from behind the dryers. The back wall glowed a brighter blue, and Furry and Flo exchanged a knowing look.

"Not again!" Flo cried. "We just got rid of the skeletons!" She hopped off the washing machine and headed for the crack. Furry followed, and together they squeezed into the space behind the dryers.

Flo gasped at what they saw. A skeletal hand reached up through the portal crack. But it didn't seem to be trying to climb out. Instead, it simply held a folded piece of paper.

Furry and Flo just stared at it for a minute. Then Furry stepped forward.

"No," Flo cried. "Don't! It's a trap!"

"No," Furry said. "I think it's a note." He reached out and snatched the paper from the bony fingers. As soon as he did, the skeletal hand slipped back into the crack and disappeared. The blue glow faded a bit, and the crack seemed to shrink slightly.

Flo stood behind Furry as he unfolded the note. Over his shoulder, she read the five, short words scratched on the paper in messy black ink:

THE AUTHOR

Thomas Kingsley Troupe writes, makes movies, and works as a firefighter/EMT. He's written many books for kids, including *Legend of the Vampire* and *Mountain Bike Hero*, and has two boys of his own. He likes zombies, bacon, orange Popsicles, and reading stories to his kids. Thomas currently lives in Woodbury, Minnesota, with his super cool family.

THE ILLUSTRATOR

Stephen Gilpin is the illustrator of several dozen children's books and is currently working on a project he hopes will give him the ability to walk through walls — although he acknowledges there is still a lot of work to be done on this project. He currently lives in Hiawatha, Kansas, with his genius wife, Angie, and their kids.

LOOK BACK AT FURRY AND FLO'S FIRST
ADVENTURE AND REMEMBER HOW IT ALL BEGAN!

THE BIG
HAIRY SECRET

The two of them sat quietly for a few
moments, then Furry spoke up. "Want to see
something awesome?" he asked.

Flo didn't want to seem too interested, but
she did like things that were awesome. "Okay,"
she said with a shrug. "I guess."

Furry led Flo over to a cramped space
behind the dryers. Rusty pipes ran overhead
and lint balls covered the floor. Near the wall,
a thin, blue line made a jagged slash across

the floor. It almost seemed to be glowing.

"What is that?" Flo asked. She couldn't pretend to be disinterested anymore. The blue line was pretty cool.

"It's a crack in the floor," Furry said.

"I see that. Why is it glowing?" Flo asked.

"How should I know?" Furry replied. He crouched down and leaned in close. The light shining from the crack bathed his face in an eerie blue light.

And just like that, Flo forgot all about the Popsicles.

CATCH UP
ON ALL FOUR OF
FURRY
AND FLO'S
ADVENTURES

FURRY AND FLO

1

THE BIG HAIRY SECRET

Thomas Kingsley Troupe

FURRY AND FLO

2

THE PROBLEMS WITH GOBLINS

Thomas Kingsley Troupe

FURRY AND FLO

3

THE MISPLACED MUMMY

Thomas Kingsley Troupe

FURRY AND FLO

4

THE SKELETONS IN CITY PARK

Thomas Kingsley Troupe

FIND MORE ADVENTURE AT
WWW.CAPSTONEKIDS.COM